MYTH & LEGENDS

MISHA VASILIEV

Idea, Drawing, Script
Misha Vasiliev

Comic Book Design
Alexander Polozhenko

The comic was created thanks to:
Elena Vasilyeva
Vasya Vasiliev
Oleg Penkovsky
Sergey Kazantsev
Artem Poberezhny
Marina Chebotareva
Alexey Chebotarev
as well as all OBLAST KOMIKSOV

Our Instagram Account: oblast_komiksov
Group in VK: https://vk.com/oblastkomiksov

ISBN: 978-93-91476-82-3
eISBN: 978-93-91476-90-8

Publisher: Pharos Books (P) Ltd.
Plot No.-55, Main Mother Dairy Road
Pandav Nagar, East Delhi-110092 (India)
Phone: +014049995474
WhatsApp: +014049995474
E-mail: sales@pharosbooks.in
Website: www.pharosbooks.in
Edition: 2021

Printed By: Sushma Book Binding House, Okhla
Industrial Area, Phase II, New Delhi-110020

Myths & Legends
Author: Misha Vasiliev

МУСО

MYCOP
Stand!

HA!
And what have you forgotten?

Frozen?

But

What is
happening here?

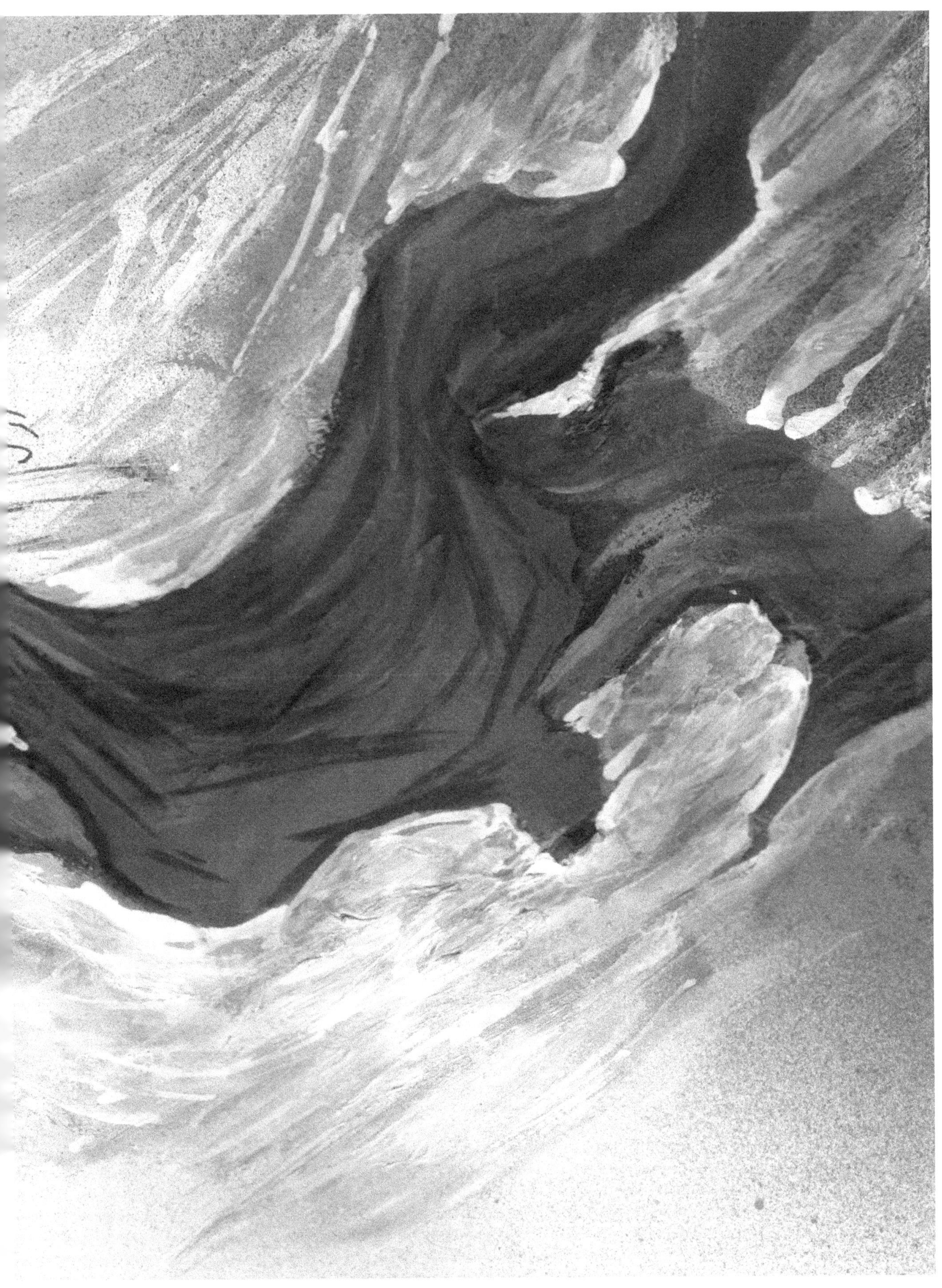

THERE ARE SUPERHEROES ALL OVER THE WORLD, EXCEPT RUSSIA.
IN AN INSTANT THEY ARE ALL SUBJECT TO A VIRAL ATTACK
THAT AFFECTS THEIR MIND, THEIR SUPERPOWER
AND TURNS THEM INTO A ZOMBIE.

WITH THE HELP OF THE ENEMEY'S INVISIBLE PORTAL THEY ARE
DISTRIBUTED ALL OVER THE WORLD.

RUSSIA, WHICH, AFTER THE COLLAPSE OF THE SOVIET UNION DID
NOT ACCEPT THE IDEA OF A SUPERMAN, TURNS OUT TO BE

THE ABSOLUTE HELP BEFORE THE APOCALYPSE.
ALMOST THE ENTIRE WORLD HAS BEEN TAKEN OVER,
BUT ONE REGION IS YET TO BE TAPPED.

IRKUTSK REGION IS THE LAST HOPE IN THE FIGHT FOR ORDER IN
THE COUNTRY.
ONLY REAL SUPERHEROES OF THE BAIKAL REGION CAN SUCCEED
AND RESTORE ORDER IN THE WORLD.

WILL THEY APPEAR?

MAYBE THIS TIME RUSSIA WILL GET AN ANSWER TO THE QUESTION
"WHO ARE RUSSIAN SUPERHEROES?"

ARE THEY MYTHS OR LEGENDS?

А
А
Я
БАИКАЛ
Say Cheese!
Cheese!

REC
Hello all! Today, we are with a group at a plein-air in Baikal.
For those who didn't know Plenair is when artists draw in nature.
REC
This is our teacher.
He's now evaluating the drawings.
Oh! Our ride has arrived. It's time to go home.
C'mon! Take every-thing back in the car. Get seated.
Well, the working day is already over. Are we going?
Vika, ride with them. I will visit my mother.
She's here in Sludyanka.
Ok. But don't forget, you're the one checking the submissions today.

BPPP
КАРЧИРИК ГАВФРРРКАП
POOOO

What
challenge
does the area
have
today?

Pooooooooooo
Quiet, Quiet, Mouse.
A birch fell on you. I will help you.
ДЫЩ!

C'mon, bear! Be of a little help.
HHH
ahmm ... is that all for today?

The girl is missing!
REFUGEE
I just want you to return home. Do you not want it?
I know you are looking for love and that means waiting.
Hey, no one will believe you.
AAAAA
Search

Kitty!

Kitty...
Meow!

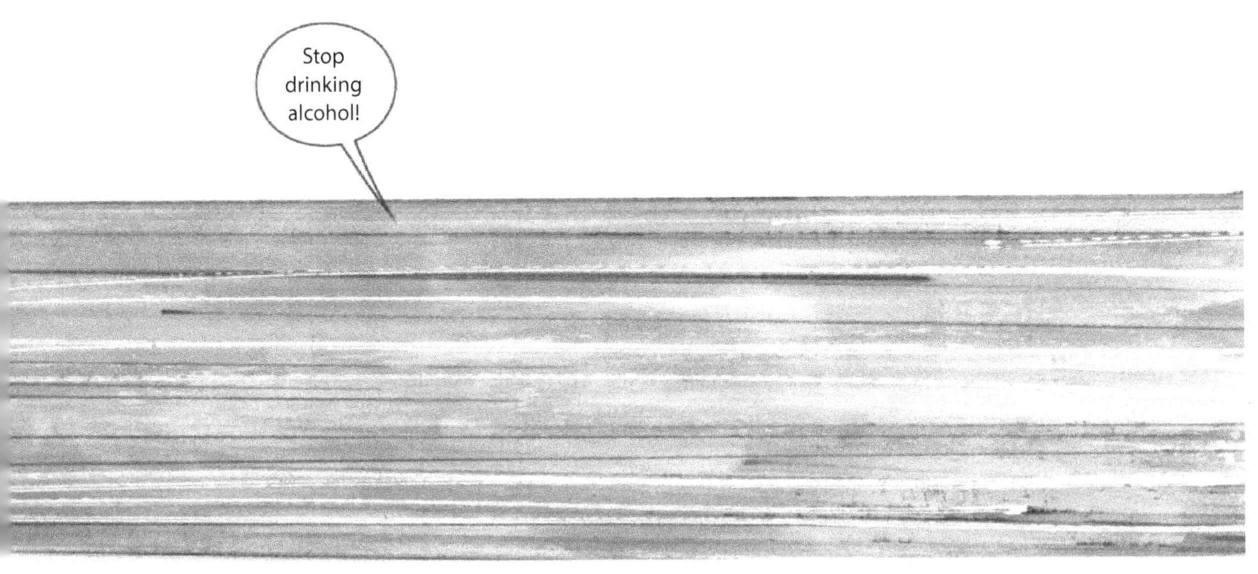
Stop drinking alcohol!

Hi,
mom.
Hi,
son.
Look at that beard! You've grown. You seem to be doing well in your town. How is your flight coming along?
Not that great. I can hardly fly up till the ceiling as if I'm chained to the ground.
This s only temporary. You'll grow.
Mom, you're a miracle. I will honour the family's name, your name. Angara is everything.
I am more worried that there is nothing to do for a superhero in Russia.
When I was young, seated on the throne of Baikal Gods, I couldn't fly either. Your grandfather, his Majesty taught me to fly.
Why don't you move to the States? There is more space for action and attitude towards superheroes is also favourable.

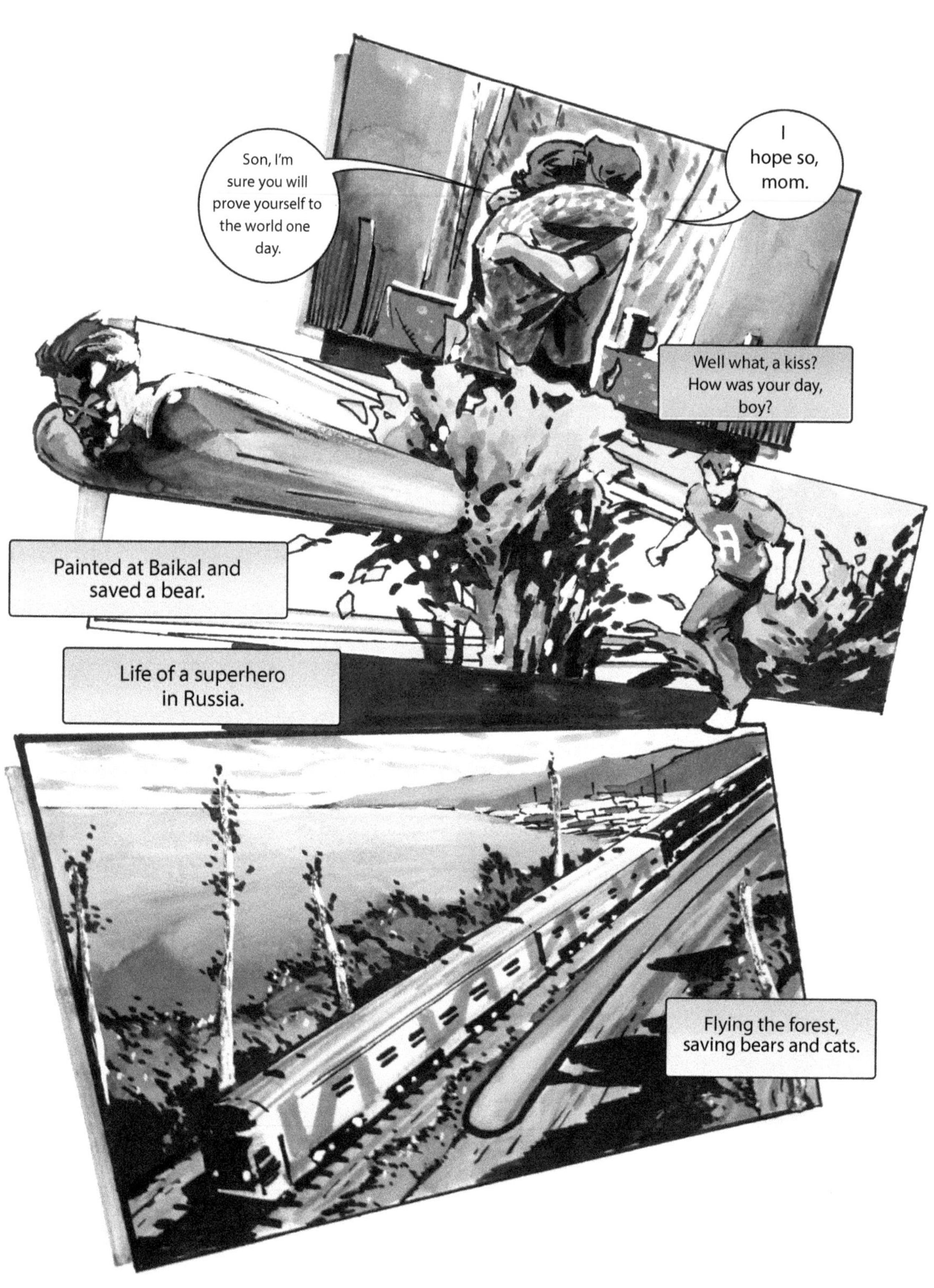
Son, I'm sure you will prove yourself to the world one day.
I hope so, mom.
Well what, a kiss? How was your day, boy?
Painted at Baikal and saved a bear.
Life of a superhero in Russia.
Flying the forest, saving bears and cats.

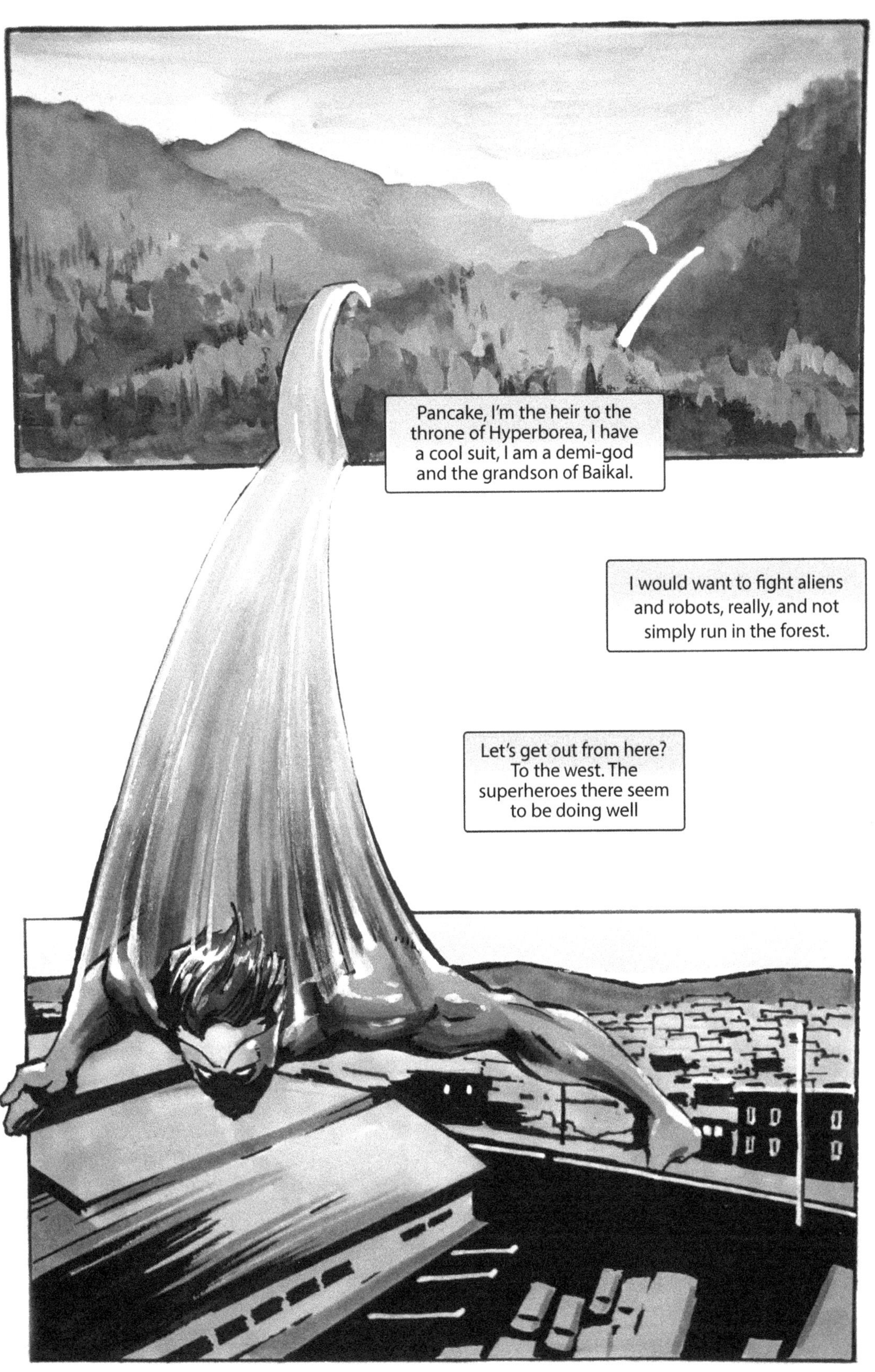
Pancake, I'm the heir to the throne of Hyperborea, I have a cool suit, I am a demi-god and the grandson of Baikal.
I would want to fight aliens and robots, really, and not simply run in the forest.
Let's get out from here? To the west. The superheroes there seem to be doing well

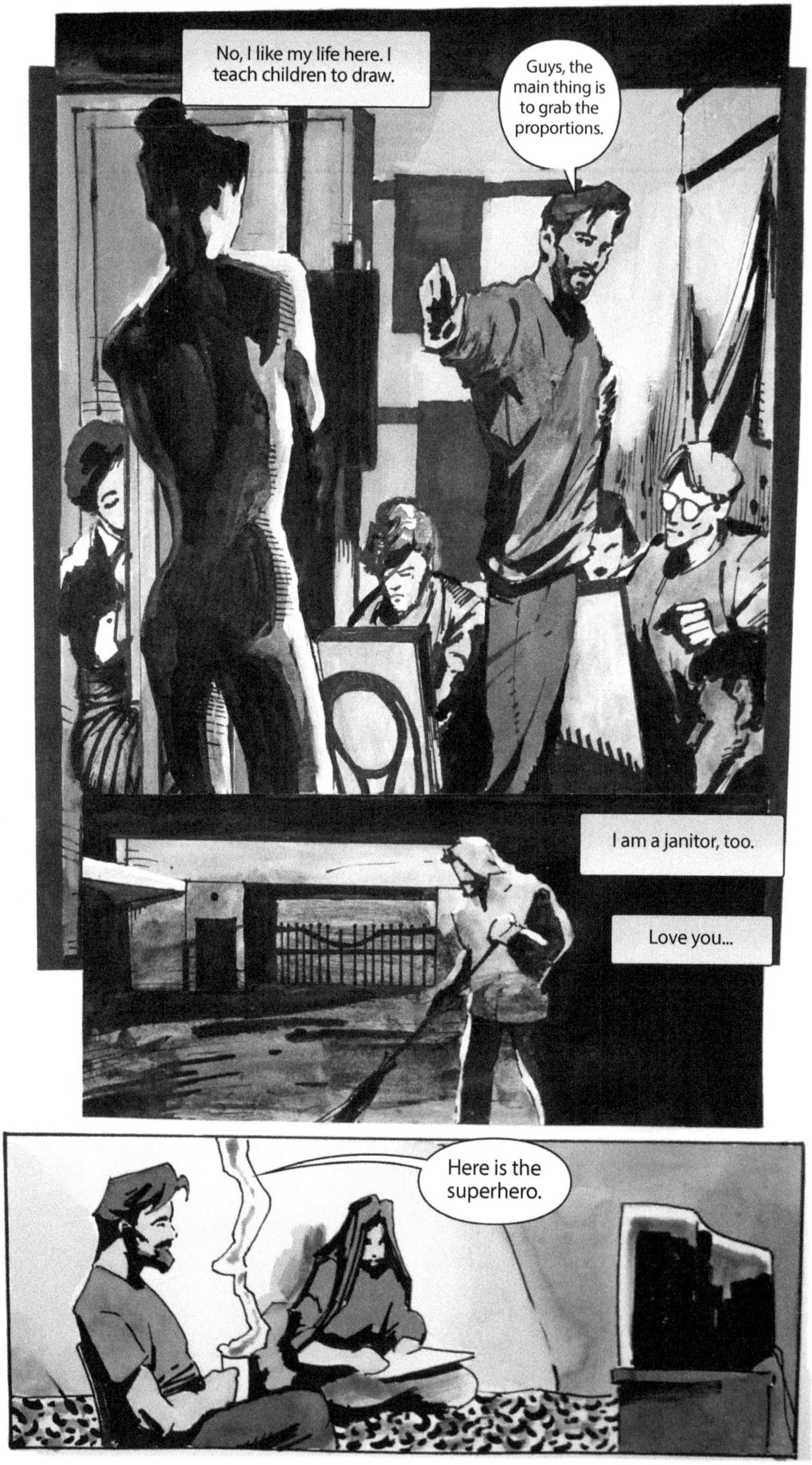

No, I like my life here. I teach children to draw.

Guys, the main thing is to grab the proportions.

I am a janitor, too.

Love you...

WE ARE INTERUPPTING THE PROGRAMME DUE
TO AN EMERGENCY NEWS.
RUSSIA HAS JUST BEEN ATTACKED BY ZOMBIE-
SUPERHEROES.
Nothing new...

Hey, are you ok man? What are you doing with Russian flag in your arms?

Uh, how did you do this? Let go of the joker!

Visibly missed you with the smoothers.

The girl is now healthy.

You are definitely not one of these.

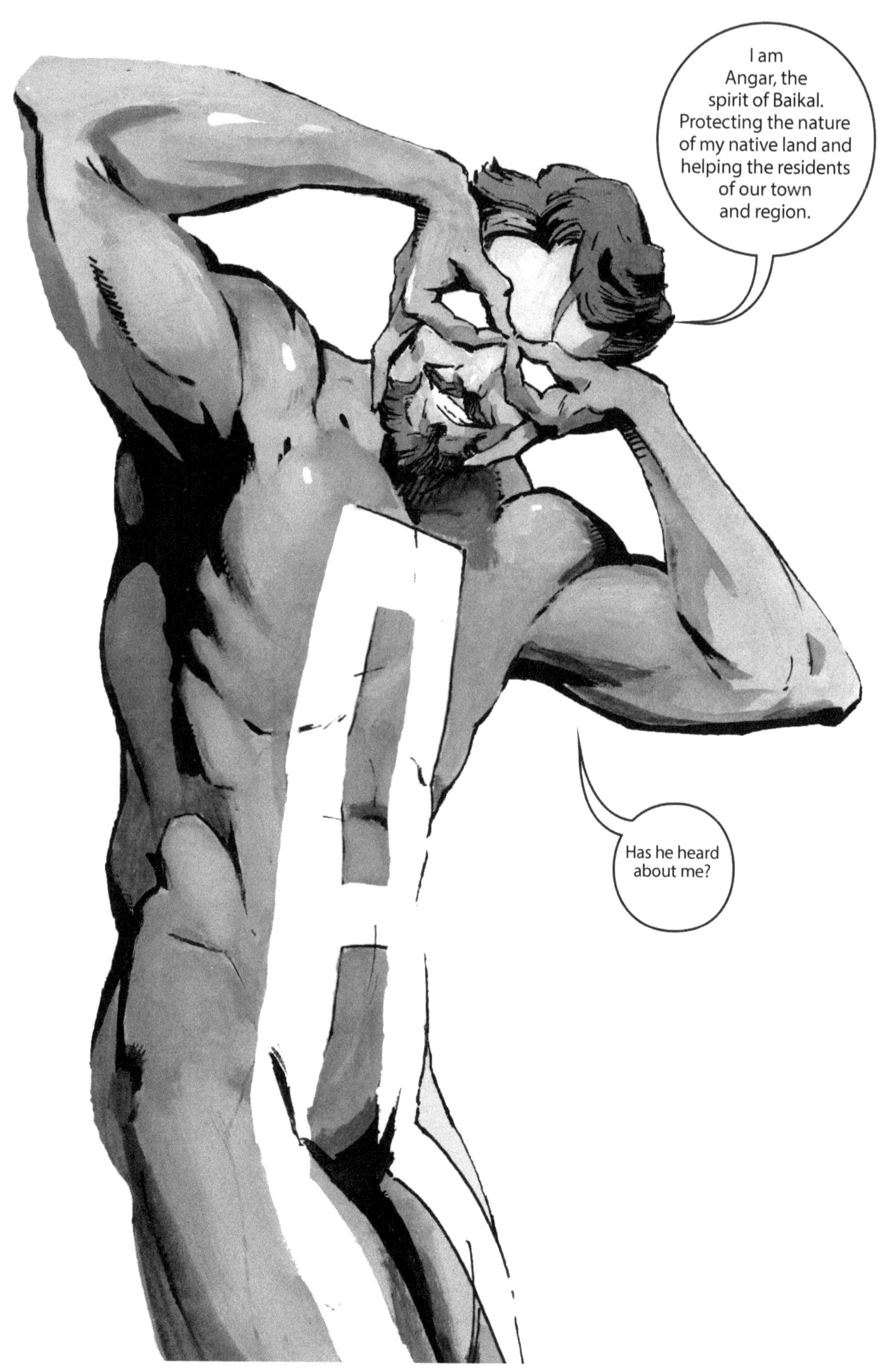
I am
Angar, the
spirit of Baikal.
Protecting the nature
of my native land and
helping the residents
of our town
and region.
Has he heard
about me?

That is the last hope of humanity, I understand.
Do you know what's happening here?
Yes, a real zombie apocalypse. Just like in the movies!
Hey, don't come back at me Miss Russia, 2021!
How do you like movies? But, if it's like a movie then there must definitely be someone behind this!

ЧУДО
Gentlemen, as you already know these are really dark times for Russia. The zombie apocalypse of superheroes has hit out country.

Because our people didn't accept the idea of a superhuman since the time of the Soviet Union, we are not ready for such trouble. In fact, we have no superheroes.

Therefore, our company, along with the defense forces of the Russian Federation, has developed a project to remove people with powerful abilities, simply to remove the infection, who we all know as foreign superheroes.
I take great pride in presenting Bam Hally's newest development...

First Russian superheroes.
Bear Man
Luck
Brownie
Sacred Solstice
And together they are...
A real Miracle!

ХЛОП ХЛОП
ХЛОП
ХЛОП ХЛОП
ХЛОП
ХЛОП
ХЛОП
ХЛОП
ХЛОП
ХЛОП ХЛОП

Well, that was cool! I hope everything is as good as the words.

Understand me, brother. That's right. Too much funds have been invested in this. A little scoot and we're aboard.

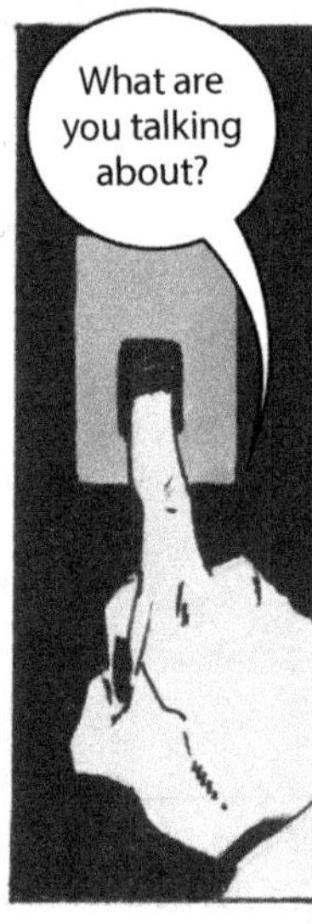
What are you talking about?

The meaning of my whole life, my childhood dream, to create my own superheroes. I put everything I have into this. There must be no errors.
This is the best!

The first Russian superhero...
TO BE CONTINUED...

НА!
И ЧЁ ВЫ ТУТ ЗАБЫЛИ?

My name is Misha Vasiliev. I'm 25 and I draw comics. After the collapse of the Soviet Union, the country changed its colours from the aggressively red Union to green, a colour of happiness, comfort and prosperity. The 90s opened access to

modern cultures of different countries for Russia with imports from the US: Spider-Man, The Mask and Batman. Who knew these would catch the imagination of a 5-year-old child from Angarsk, Irkutsk region? This is how my conquest began.

www.ingramcontent.com/pod-product-compliance
Ingram Content Group UK Ltd.
Pitfield, Milton Keynes, MK11 3LW, UK
UKHW062000290726
14090UKWH00021B/1308